Pictorial

PILGRIM'S

PROGRESS

Pictorial

PILGRIM'S PROGRESS

MOODY PRESS

CHICAGO

ISBN 0-8024-0019-1
Twenty-eighth Printing, 1982

Printed in the United States of America

INTRODUCTION

IN THE REIGN of James II of England, popular Protestant preacher John Bunyan (1628-1688) was arrested for "holding unlawful assemblies and not conforming to the national worship of the church of England." Because he refused to conform, he was cast into Bedford Jail in 1660 where he remained twelve years.

Content to suffer for his belief, he spent his time in the study of the Word of God, which began to shine with greater glory than ever. Parting from his wife and children was for him "like pulling the flesh from the bones," and the knowledge that they were suffering hardships "nearly broke his heart." Still he determined to "venture them all with God."

While he lingered in what he called "this lions' den," he longed after his congregation who were his children in the Lord. In hope of strengthening their faith, he took his pen, and while writing,

> Fell suddenly into an allegory,
> About their journey and the way to glory,
> In more than twenty things which I set down.
> This done, I twenty more had in my crown;
> And they again began to multiply,
> Like sparks that from the coals of fire do fly.

The result was *The Pilgrim's Progress,* now known as the world's most famous allegory. In this book the old story is recast into pictorial forms for the instruction and pleasure of both young and old.

I dreamed I saw a man with a burden on his back.

As I walked through the wilderness of this world, I came upon a place where there was a Den. There I lay down to sleep; as I slept I dreamed a dream.

I saw a man clothed in rags, his face turned away from his home, a Book in his hand, and a great burden on his back (Isa. 64:6). I looked and saw him open the Book and read; as he read he wept and trembled. Unable to contain his grief, he broke out in a lamentable cry, "What shall I do?" (Acts 2:37).

The man tells his trouble to his family.

In this plight he went home and tried to conceal his grief, not wanting his wife and children to see his distress. But he could not be silent. Finally he poured out his heart to them: "O my dear wife and beloved children. I am in great trouble because of a heavy load pressing down on me. I am told that this city in which we live will be burned by fire from Heaven. If we are caught in that disaster we shall all perish, unless we first find some way of escape."

8

His family thinks he is losing his mind.

His wife and children were amazed and frightened, not that they believed him, but because they thought he was losing his mind. Since it was toward evening, they urged him to go to bed, hoping that a good night's sleep might settle his mind.

He is so restless he cannot sleep.
The night was as troublesome as the day. He was so restless he couldn't sleep, but spent the whole night in sighs and tears.

10

"How do you feel this morning?"

In the morning when his wife and children came in to ask how he felt, he answered, "Worse and worse." Then he repeated his fears of the previous day, but they refused to listen.

They treat him harshly.

They ridiculed him and rebuked him. Sometimes
they ignored him completely.

He goes to his bedroom and prays for them.
Having endured this cruel treatment for some
time, he went back to his room. Lamenting his own
misery and grieving at his family's behavior, he
prayed God to have compassion on them.

13

Greatly distressed, he walks alone in the fields.

For several days he walked in the fields, sometimes reading his Book, sometimes praying, but always greatly distressed. As he read he cried aloud, "What must I do to be saved?" He looked this way and that as if he wanted to run; yet he stood still, because he could not decide which way to go.

He meets Evangelist.

I saw a man named Evangelist come to him and ask, "Why do you cry?"

He answered, "Sir, I read in this book that I must die, and after death come to judgment. I do not want to die, and I dare not face the judgment."

"Since life is so full of trouble, why are you not willing to die?" asked Evangelist.

"Because I fear that this burden on my back will sink me lower than the grave and I shall fall into Hell."

15

Evangelist gives him a scroll.

"If you are in such trouble, why do you stay here?" asked Evangelist.

"Because I know not where to go."

Then Evangelist gave him a parchment scroll on which were the words, "Flee from the wrath to come" (Matt. 3:7). When he saw the words he turned to Evangelist and asked, "Whither shall I flee?"

Evangelist points to a *narrow gate.

Evangelist stretched out his hand and pointed beyond the plain, saying, "Do you see that narrow gate?"

"No," he replied.

"Do you see that shining light?"

"I do seem to see a light," he answered.

Then said Evangelist, "Fix your eyes on the light, go straight toward it, and you will find the gate. When you knock on the gate, you will be told what to do next."

*The compiler uses *Narrow Gate* because the word *wicket* means *small gate*, and is not generally used today.

The man leaves his home to find the narrow gate.

In my dream I saw that the man, obedient to Evangelist's words, began to run. Before he had gone very far, his wife and children began calling after him to return. But the man put his fingers in his ears and ran on, crying, "Life! Life! Eternal life!" He looked not behind, but fled out of the city toward the middle of the plain.

His neighbors watch him and call to him.

The neighbors also came out to see him run; and as he ran, some laughed at him, others tried to frighten him, and still others called him to come back. Among them were two that resolved to bring him back by force. The name of the one was Obstinate; the other, Pliable.

Pliable and Obstinate run after him.

They urge him to return.

Christian, for that was the man's name, asked them, "Good neighbors, why have you followed me?"

"We came to urge you to return with us."

"That can never be," he replied. "You live in the City of Destruction, and I know that that city will be destroyed with fire. If you remain there you will be destroyed with it. My good neighbors, come along with me."

"And leave our friends and comforts behind?" said Obstinate.

"Yes," Christian replied, "that is just what I ask you to do. The friends and pleasures of which you speak cannot compare with the joys which I seek. And if you are willing to go along with me and remain steadfast, you will receive all that I do."

"What are the things you seek?"

Obstinate asked, "What are the things you seek, since you are willing to leave all the world to find them?"

"I seek an inheritance incorruptible and unde-filed, that fadeth not away," said Christian (I Peter 1:4). "It is safely laid up in Heaven, and any man who diligently seeks it will receive it. Read this book and you will understand."

"Tush!" said Obstinate. "Away with your Book! Will you go back with us or not?"

"No," answered Christian. "I have already laid my hand to the plough, and I will not turn back."

Obstinate accuses Christian of insanity.

"Come, neighbor Pliable," Obstinate urged, "let us go home without him. This crazy person is full of empty words. He thinks he is clever and no one is his equal."

But Pliable answered, "Don't make fun of him. Christian is a good man. If what he says is true, I think I shall go with him."

"What! More fools still?" exclaimed Obstinate in disgust. "You had better come along with me. Who knows where this crazy fellow will take you? Come back! Don't be a fool!"

Christian pleads, but Obstinate refuses to listen.

Christian pleaded with Obstinate, "Don't tell him to go back! Both of you come along with me. The happiness and glory I spoke of are real. If you don't believe me, just read what is written in this Book. Every word is true. The writer of the Book shed His blood for a token."

Then Pliable said to Obstinate, "Friend, I think I will go along with this good man and endure hardship with him." Turning to Christian, he said, "Friend, do you know the way to the place you seek?"

"Evangelist showed me that beyond this plain there is a narrow gate," Christian replied. "When we get there someone will tell us what road to take next."

"Good!" said Pliable. "Let us both be on our way."

Obstinate returns home.

"I will not be companion to such crazy, ignorant people," said Obstinate. "I'm going home."

In my dream I saw Christian and Pliable slowly proceed over the plain, walking and talking together.

CHRISTIAN: Neighbor Pliable, I am so glad you listened to me and came along. If Obstinate had felt the powers and terrors of the unseen as I have, he would not so lightly have turned back.

PLIABLE: Now that you and I are alone, neighbor Christian, tell me more about the place where we are going. What kind of pleasures are there and how are they to be enjoyed?

CHRISTIAN: This matter I can feel better with my heart than explain with my lips. But since you wish to understand, I will read you the words of the Book.

The two men walk along together.

PLIABLE: Do you think the words of the Book are true?

CHRISTIAN: Certainly, for it was written by Him who cannot lie.

PLIABLE: Tell me, what does it say?

CHRISTIAN: There is an eternal kingdom where death cannot enter and where we shall live forever.

PLIABLE: And what else?

CHRISTIAN: Crowns of glory will be given us, and garments that will make us shine like the sun.

PLIABLE: That is wonderful! And what else?

CHRISTIAN: In that place there is no sorrow nor crying. The Lord of that land will wipe away all tears from our eyes (Rev. 21:4).

PLIABLE: Who will be our companions?

CHRISTIAN: Heavenly creatures whose brightness will dazzle our eyes. Also thousands and ten thousands who have gone before us. Everyone there is pure in heart, loving and holy.

As they talk they come to the Slough of Despond.

CHRISTIAN: Many of the saints in that kingdom have suffered at the hands of the world because of their love and obedience to the Lord. Some had been cut to pieces, some had been burned in the fire, some had been drowned, and others eaten by beasts. But now they are all clothed with immortality as with a garment.

PLIABLE: What you say thrills me, but how are these things to be enjoyed? How are we to share them?

CHRISTIAN: The Lord has written in the Book that if we are willing to ask Him He will freely give them to us.

PLIABLE: I am glad to hear all this. Come on, let us make haste to get there.

CHRISTIAN: I cannot go so fast because of the burden on my back.

Then in my dream I saw that they drew near to the Slough of Despond, a very miry bog in the middle of the plain.

They fall into the Slough.

Busily talking and heedless of the way, they both
fell suddenly into the bog. In this mire they wal-
lowed around till their clothes were covered with
mud. Because of the burden on his back, Christian
began to sink.

"How did we get into this mess?" asked Pliable.

Christian replied, "Truly, I do not know."

Beginning to be offended, Pliable said angrily,
"Is this the happiness of which you spoke?"

Pliable returns home in anger.

PLIABLE: If we have had such a bad beginning, who knows what dangers we shall run into before the journey is over? If I get out of this with my life, you may possess that brave land alone for all I care.

At this he turned back. Struggling desperately, he climbed out of the mire on the side where they had fallen in and returned to his home. Christian saw him no more.

Christian cannot get out.

Left to struggle in the Slough of Despond alone, poor Christian dragged himself through to the side which was nearest the narrow gate. But he could not climb out because of the burden on his back, and he began to sink again. Then I saw in my dream that a man named Help came along.

Help pulls Christian out of the mire.

"What are you doing here?" Help asked Christian.

He replied, "A man named Evangelist directed me to yonder narrow gate that I might escape the wrath to come. As I was on my way I fell into the mud."

"But why didn't you look?" Help asked. "There are stone steps set in the mire by which you could have crossed over safely."

"I was in a hurry to get to the narrow gate, so I took the nearest way," Christian explained. "That is why I fell in."

Then said Help, "Give me your hand. Taking Christian by the hand, he pulled him out and set him on solid ground.

The source of the Slough of Despond.

Standing beside Help, Christian asked, "Since the road from the City of Destruction to the narrow gate leads this way, why is this bog not filled in, so that travelers might go over in safety?"

"This miry pit cannot be easily mended," Help replied. "As a man becomes aware of his sin, all the old dregs and filth from his heart flow down here. That is why it is called the Slough of Despond. When a sinner realizes he is lost, fears and doubts arise in his soul, all of which settle here and make it an evil ground. Still it is not the King's wish that this place remain bad. For more than 1900 years workmen have been trying to mend it."

Help points out the stepping stones.

Help also said to Christian, "By order of the King, good and solid steps have been placed evenly through the slough, but when it rains and the mire casts up its filth, these steps are barely visible. Even if they can be seen, men often become dizzy, lose their footing and slip into the mire. However, at the narrow gate the ground becomes solid again."

Doubting Pliable reaches home.

Then in my dream I saw that Pliable had already reached home, and his friends came to see him. Some said he showed wisdom in returning. Some called him a fool for venturing to go with Christian. Still others mocked his cowardice, saying, "Once you began the journey, why did you give up because of a few difficulties?" At first Pliable sat sneakingly among them, afraid to lift his head. But after a while he got back his confidence and started to make fun of poor Christian.

Christian meets Worldly Wiseman.

Then Christian went on his way, walking by himself, until he saw someone in the distance coming toward him through the fields. This man was a very learned gentleman named Worldly Wiseman who lived in the town of Carnal Policy (Worldly Wisdom), a very great town not far from Christian's own home.

They start to talk.

Seeing Christian groaning and sighing under his heavy burden, Worldly Wiseman asked, "Where are you going in such a burdensome manner, my good fellow?"

CHRISTIAN: A burdensome manner indeed! I don't think there is anyone in the whole world more burdensome than I. You ask where I am going? Over there to yonder narrow gate. I have heard that someone lives there who will tell me how to get rid of my burden.

WORLDLY WISEMAN: Have you a wife and children?

CHRISTIAN: Yes. But because of this heavy burden pressing me down, I cannot take pleasure in them as formerly, and I feel as if I had none.

Worldly Wiseman's advice.

WORLDLY WISEMAN: I have some good advice for you. Do you want to listen?

CHRISTIAN: I never refuse to listen to good advice.

WORLDLY WISEMAN: Then I advise you to get rid of that burden quickly. Until you do so you will never be at ease in your mind or able to enjoy the blessings God has given you.

CHRISTIAN: That is just what I am looking for — a way to get rid of this burden! But I cannot do it myself, nor is anyone in my town able to help me. I am going this way to find out where I can get rid of it.

WORLDLY WISEMAN: Who told you you could get rid of it by going this road?

CHRISTIAN: A man named Evangelist.

WORLDLY WISEMAN: Pooh! That was very wicked advice to give you. There is no more dangerous road in all the world! You may not believe me now, but you will find out later.

Wicked Worldly Wiseman deceives Christian.

WORLDLY WISEMAN: I see you have already met with trouble. Your clothes are covered with the mud of the Slough of Despond and yet you are still going this way. That was only the beginning of trouble for you. Hear me, I am older than you. On this road you will meet with weariness, pain, hunger, cold, sword, wild beasts, darkness and death. Why listen to a stranger and throw away your life?

Christian is almost persuaded.

WORLDLY WISEMAN: How did you come by this heavy burden at first?

CHRISTIAN: By reading this Book in my hand.

WORLDLY WISEMAN: I thought as much. Weak men like yourself who meddle with things too high for them become confused. They are filled with so many doubts and fears that they run around on desperate adventures without even knowing what they are after.

CHRISTIAN: But I do know what I want. I want to get rid of this burden.

WORLDLY WISEMAN: But this road you are taking is very dangerous. If you want to be at ease, why did you come here? If you will hear me patiently, I will not only tell you how to obtain what you seek and avoid this dangerous road, but how to get rid of your burden as well. My words will not only save you from distress, but will bring you safety, happiness and contentment.

Christian is now taken in and believes Worldly Wiseman.

CHRISTIAN: Sir, I pray, reveal this secret to me.

WORLDLY WISEMAN: Well now, that's better. In yonder village of Morality there is a very learned man named Legality. He is very clever, very well thought of, and has skill to help men get rid of such burdens as yours. He has done a great deal of good in this way. Besides, he can help those whose minds are upset because of their troubles. If he is not at home, he has a fine young son named Civility who is just as clever as the old gentleman himself. There you will be quite happy and free of your burden. If you do not want to return to your old home — (as indeed I would not advise) you can send for your wife and children to live in the village of Morality. There are many empty houses, the rent is reasonable, and the food is good and cheap. The neighbors are all honest, respectable and dependable, so your life will be safe and happy.

Christian leaves the road.

Christian finally concluded that if these persuasive words were true, the wisest course was to follow the advice of Worldly Wiseman. So he asked, "Which is the way to this honest man's house?"

Worldly Wiseman, pointing to a high hill not far away, asked, "Do you see yonder high hill?"

CHRISTIAN: Yes, very well.

WORLDLY WISEMAN: Go by way of that hill; the first house you will come to is his.

So Christian turned out of the way to go to Mr Legality's house for help.

At the foot of the hill he is afraid.

When he reached the high hill, he saw that an overhanging cliff threatened to topple over on the road, and he was afraid to venture farther lest the rocks fall on his head. So he stood still, not knowing what to do. His burden now seemed much heavier than before. Flashes of lightning came forth from the hill, and Christian, thinking he would be burned alive, trembled and sweated with fear.

Christian sees Evangelist coming and is ashamed.

He was begining to feel sorry he had taken Mr. Worldly Wiseman's counsel when he saw Evangelist coming to meet him, and he blushed for shame. Evangelist drew near and, looking on Christian with a severe and dreadful countenance, asked, "What are you doing here, Christian?" Christian knew not what to answer, and stood speechless before him.

"Why did you turn aside?"

Then said Evangelist, "Are you not the man I found crying outside the walls of the City of Destruction?"

CHRISTIAN: Yes, I am the man.

EVANGELIST: Did I not direct you to the narrow gate?

CHRISTIAN: Yes.

EVANGELIST: How is it then that you are so quickly turned aside?

CHRISTIAN: Right after I had gotten out of the Slough of Despond, I met a gentleman who persuaded me that I might find a man in the village before me who could take off my burden.

EVANGELIST: Who was he?

CHRISTIAN: He looked like a gentleman and talked to me until I yielded. So I came here. But when I got to this hill I was afraid it would fall on my head, so I dared not go forward lest I be crushed to death.

Evangelist continues to question Christian.

EVANGELIST: What did this man say to you?

CHRISTIAN: He asked where I was going, and I told him.

EVANGELIST: And what did he say then?

CHRISTIAN: He asked if I had a family. I said I had, but that I was so weighed down by this burden on my back I could not enjoy them as I used to do.

EVANGELIST: And what did he say then?

CHRISTIAN: He told me to get rid of my burden quickly. When I told him I was going to the narrow gate to get directions to the place of deliverance, he said he would show me a better and a shorter way, one not so attended with difficulties as the way you set me in. So I believed him and turned out of the right way and came here in the hope of getting rid of my burden sooner. But when I got here and saw things as they are, I stopped for fear. Now I don't know what to do.

Evangelist sternly rebukes Christian.

EVANGELIST: Stand still a while and listen, that I may show you the words of God.

Christian stood trembling as Evangelist read from the Word: "See that ye refuse not him that speaketh. For if they escaped not who refused him that spake on earth, much more shall not we escape, if we turn away from him that speaketh from heaven" (Heb. 12:25). He said moreover, "Now the just shall live by faith: but if any man draw back, my soul shall have no pleasure in him" (Heb. 10:38). Evangelist then applied these words to Christian. "You have turned aside from the way of peace into this danger-ous place and almost lost your life."

Christian bitterly repents.

Hearing these words, Christian fell down and cried out, "Woe is me, for I am undone!"

But Evangelist caught him by the hand, saying, "All manner of sin and blasphemies shall be forgiven unto men. Be not faithless but believing (cf. Matt. 12:31; John 20:27). Christian revived and stood trembling before Evangelist. Evangelist continued, "Give more earnest heed to the things I am going to show you. I will show you who it was that deluded you and to whom he sent you. The man that met you is Worldly Wiseman. He is well named, because he is worldly and he loves morality and the laying up of virtue. He will not listen to the teaching of the cross and salvation."

Three errors in Worldly Wiseman's advice.

There were three errors in Worldly Wiseman's advice: he turned you out of the true way; he tried to make the cross odious to you; he sent you on the way that leads to death.

48

Christian laments his folly.

Christian thought the hour of death had come and he cried, "I was a fool to listen to Worldly Wiseman and forsake the right way!"

49

Evangelist points him back to the right way.

Then Evangelist pointed out the way back to the road leading to the narrow gate and warned him not to be fooled again.

In penitence Christian decides to go back.
When Christian said he would go back, Evangelist
smiled and bade him Godspeed.

Christian hastens to return.

As Christian hurried back, he carefully avoided speaking to anybody he met on the road. He was like one treading on forbidden ground, not feeling safe until he was back on the right way.

Christian arrives at the narrow gate.

When Christian arrived at the narrow gate, he saw written above it the words: "Knock, and it shall be opened unto you" (Matt. 7:7). So he went up and knocked.

Goodwill opens the gate.

At last a solemn man named Goodwill opened the gate and asked, "Who are you? Where did you come from? What do you want?"

Christian answered, "I am a poor burdened sinner from the City of Destruction. I am going to Mount Zion that I may be delivered from the wrath to come."

Goodwill pulls Christian inside.

Then Goodwill quickly pulled Christian inside. "Why did you do that?" asked Christian.

"A little distance from this gate is the **Devil's Castle**," said Goodwill. "He watches all those who come here and shoots arrows at them. Some unfortunate people are killed by his arrows and never get inside."

Christian rejoices upon entering the narrow gate.

Then said Christian, "I rejoice and tremble."

"Who directed you here?" asked Goodwill.

Then Christian described all that had happened on the way.

Goodwill shows Christian the straight and narrow way.

Goodwill listened attentively and then said, "Come over here with me and I will show you the next road you must take. Look before you. Do you see that straight road? That is the way you must go. It was built by the prophets of old and by Christ and His disciples. On either side there are many winding paths that are crooked and wide. Only the right road is straight and narrow. Follow it and you will come to the Interpreter's house. Knock at his door and he will show you many wonderful things.

*Christian follows the straight road to the
Interpreter's house.*

Christian set out to walk the straight road. When
he reached the Interpreter's house, he knocked again
and again. At last someone came and asked, "Who
are you?"

"I would speak to the master of the house," Christian replied.

When the Interpreter appeared, Christian explained that Goodwill had sent him.

"I will show you much."

Then said the Interpreter, "Come in, and I will show you much that will be profitable to you. Bidding his servant light a candle, he took Christian into a private room.

A picture of a very serious man.

Here he saw the picture of a very serious person standing as if to plead with men. His eyes were lifted to Heaven, and he had the best of books in his hand. On his head was a crown of gold, and the world was behind him.

"This man," the Interpreter explained, "can transform people and cause them to be born again. The world behind his back and the crown on his head show that he who despises the things of this world may enjoy the blessings of Heaven."

Christian learns of two ways to sweep a hall.

The Interpreter next took Christian into a large hall that was full of dust because it had never been swept. After they had looked at it for a moment, the Interpreter called for a man to sweep. As he swept, the dust rose in such clouds that Christian was almost choked. The Interpreter then told a maiden who stood by, "Bring water and sprinkle the room." The room was then swept clean.

The meaning of the dusty room.

"What does this mean?" asked Christian.

The Interpreter answered, "This hall is the heart of man; the dust is the sin that has defiled him. He that began to sweep at first is the Law; she that brought water and sprinkled it is the Gospel. The Law, instead of cleansing the heart from sin, only revives and increases sin in the soul. But when the sweet and precious influences of the Gospel come in, sin is vanquished and the soul made clean and fit for the King of glory to inhabit."

Passion and Patience.

In my dream I saw the Interpreter take Christian by the hand and lead him into a little room where two children sat. The name of the one was Passion; the other, Patience. Passion seemed discontented, but Patience was very quiet. Christian inquired, "Why is Passion so discontented?"

The Interpreter answered, "His parents have told him to wait until next year for the best things. He wants them now, so he is vexed. But Patience is willing to wait."

63

The bag of treasure.

Then I saw someone bring Passion a bag of treasure and pour it at his feet. Laughing triumphantly at Patience, he picked up the treasure. But in a short time he had wasted it all and had nothing left but rags.

The Interpreter's explanation.

So the Interpreter said, "Passion is a figure of the men of this world; Patience, of the men of the world to come. Just as Passion wanted all his pleasures now, the men of this world must have all their good things now; they are not willing to wait for life after death. And as Passion's treasures were speedily wasted away, so it will be with those who seek the happiness that this world offers."

Christian sees an unquenchable fire.

Then the Interpreter took Christian by the hand and led him to a place where there was a fire burning against a wall. A man stood by, continuously pouring water upon it, but the fire only burned brighter and hotter.

Then said Christian, "What does this mean?"

The Interpreter answered, "The fire is the work of grace in the human heart. He that pours water upon it to put it out is the devil. But, as you see, the fire only burns brighter and hotter. I will show you the reason for that."

He learns why the fire does not go out.

Then the Interpreter took Christian behind the wall. Here he saw another man with a vessel in his hand continually pouring oil upon the fire.

"What does this mean?" Christian asked.

The Interpreter answered, "This is Christ. He uses the oil of His grace to keep up the work already begun in the heart of His people. Christ's own people are children of grace, and the devil's power, though great, cannot quench the work of grace begun in their heart. As you see, this man stands behind the wall; that is to teach you that it is hard for those who are tempted to see how this work of grace is kept up in their souls."

He sees a gateway guarded by four men in armor.

Next the Interpreter led Christian to a very beautiful and imposing gateway with four strong men in armor standing in front. At the side of the gateway, a man sat behind a desk on which he kept a book in which to write the names of any who should enter. In front of the gateway stood a large group of people who seemed anxious to enter, but they were afraid of the armed men. On the walls of the palace a great company of people clothed in white robes stood watching.

A brave warrior fights his way in.

However, no one seemed brave enough to risk
the fight. At last Christian saw a very courageous
man go up to the scribe, saying, "Write down my
name, sir." When this was done, he put a helmet
on his head and drew his sword, then boldly rushed
forward to fight the four men in armor. They fought
him with deadly force. But, slashing and hacking his
way most fiercely, and giving and receiving many
wounds, he succeeded in cutting his way into the
palace.

A chorus greets him.

At this a chorus of happy voices was heard singing:

Come in, come in;
Eternal glory thou shalt win.

So he went in and was clothed in white garments like theirs.

"I think I know the meaning of this," said Christian, smiling. "Now let me go on my way."

The man in the iron cage.

"No, wait," said the Interpreter, "till I have shown you a little more, and after that you shall go on your way." So he took him by the hand and led him to a very dark room where a man sat in an iron cage. This man seemed very sorrowful. He sat with his eyes downcast, his hands folded together, and he sighed as if his heart would break.

"What does this mean?" asked Christian.

"You may ask the man yourself," the Interpreter replied.

The man explains the reason for his misery.
Christian walked up to the iron cage and asked,
"Who are you?"

"I once appeared to be a good and successful Christian. I thought I was on the way to the Celestial City and was happy at the thought of getting there.

"But what are you now?"

"Now I am a man of despair because I left off to watch and be sober and gave rein to my lusts. I sinned against the light of the Word and goodness of God. I tempted the devil, and he is come to me. I have grieved the Spirit, and He is gone. I have so hardened my heart that I cannot repent."

"But can you not now repent and return?"

"God hath denied me repentance. Alas, He has shut me in this cage. O eternity! Eternity! How shall I endure eternal punishment?"

Interpreter warns Christian.

Then said the Interpreter to Christian, "Let this man's misery be remembered by you and be your warning."

"This is fearful," said Christian. "May God help me to be sober. Sir, I pray thee, let me go on my way now."

The man who shook and trembled.

But the Interpreter said, "Wait till I show you one more thing and then you shall go on your way." He took Christian to a bedroom where a man was rising out of bed. As he put on his clothes, he shook and trembled.

Then said Christian, "Why does this man tremble?" The Interpreter bade the man tell Christian the reason.

"I had a dream," said the man.

The man tells his dream.

"Last night in my sleep I dreamed that the heavens grew very black and it thundered and lightened. I looked up and saw a man sitting on a cloud, attended by thousands of angels. I also heard a voice saying, 'Arise ye dead and come to judgment!' With that the dead came out of their graves, some full of joy and some full of fear. He that sat upon the cloud bade the angels, 'Cast the tares and the stubble into the lake of fire' (Matt. 3:12; 13:40; Rev. 20: 12, 15)."

The bottomless pit.

"The bottomless pit opened where I stood, and out of its mouth came forth fire and smoke. I thought the day of judgment had come and I was not ready, and I was terrified."

Christian goes on his way singing.

After Christian had seen these spiritual lessons, he said farewell. The Interpreter bade him Godspeed, saying, "The Comforter be always with you, good Christian, to guide you in the way that leads to the City." So Christian set out again singing.

The wall of Salvation.

Now I saw in my dream that the highway which Christian traveled was fenced in on either side with a wall called Salvation. Up this way Christian ran, but with great difficulty because of the burden on his back.

*Christian comes to the cross and
the load falls off his back.*

Christian ran thus till he came to a high place,
on top of which stood a wooden cross, and below
that an empty grave. As he came up to the cross, his
burden fell off his shoulders and rolled into the
mouth of the grave, and I saw it no more. Then was
Christian wondrously relieved and said with a merry
heart, "He has given me rest by His sorrow and life
by His death."

He gazes in wonder.

Amazed that the sight of the cross should ease him of his burden, he stood gazing in wonder. Tears came to his eyes and rolled down his cheeks.

Three Shining Ones appear.

As he stood there looking and weeping, behold,
three Shining Ones came and saluted him, saying,
"Peace be with you." The first said, "Your sins are all
forgiven." The second stripped him of his rags and
clothed him with a new white robe. The third set
a mark upon his forehead and gave him a scroll with
a seal upon it, bidding him read it as he ran and
hand it in when he reached the Celestial Gate.

*Christian goes on his way, leaping and
singing for joy.*

He meets Simple, Sloth and Presumption.

I saw then that he went on down the hill. Near the bottom, on the edge of a cliff, three men lay fast asleep with iron fetters on their legs. The name of the one was Simple; another, Sloth; and the third, Presumption.

Christian warns them of their danger.

Seeing them lying thus, Christian went to waken them and warn them of their danger. "Beware! Beneath you is a gulf that has no bottom! Come away, and I will help you off with your irons."

But they said, "We see no danger," and lay down to sleep again. Christian had no choice but to go on his way, but he was troubled that they did not see their danger.

He meets Formalist and Hypocrisy.

As he thought on these things, two men, Formalist and Hypocrisy, came tumbling over the wall on the left hand of the narrow way. As they drew near, Christian asked, "Gentlemen, where did you come from and where are you going?"

They replied, "We were born in the land of Vainglory and are going to seek fame and fortune in the Celestial City."

He asks why they came in over the wall.

Christian replied, "You say you want to go to the Celestial City and yet you climbed over the wall instead of entering by the narrow gate. You have already disobeyed the law of the land and the Lord of the Celestial City will not allow you to enter."

The two answered, "Our way is shorter; besides, it is the custom for our countrymen to enter this way. You came in by the narrow gate, we climbed over the wall; yet we are all traveling along the same road."

But Christian answered, "I walk by the rule of the Lord. You walk by the rule of your own hearts. You are already counted as thieves by the Lord of the way."

They go on in their own way.

The pair made no answer to this except to say,
"We will go our way, and you yours." So they went
on, every man in his own way.

Formalist and Hypocrisy argue with Christian.

After a while Formalist and Hypocrisy began to argue with Christian, saying, "We keep all the law just as you do. The only difference between us is that coat on your back. Perhaps that is to cover up the shame of your nakedness!"

Christian replies.

"This coat was given me by the Lord of the city, and when I come to the gate He will know me by the coat He gave me. I have a mark upon my forehead, and also a sealed scroll which I am to hand over when I go in at the Celestial gate. I doubt if you have these things, because you did not come in through the narrow gate."

To this they gave no answer; they just looked at each other and laughed.

Ahead — the Hill Difficulty.

The three went on till they came to the Hill Difficulty, at the foot of which was a spring of water.
Here were also two roads. One turned to the right
and the other to the left, but the narrow way led
between them straight up to the top of the hill.

Christian laps water.

Christian went to the spring and drank some water. This refreshed him so that he eagerly began to climb the hill by way of the narrow road.

Formalist and Hypocrisy also came to the foot of the hill, but when they looked up to its towering summit, they decided to take the side roads. One took the way of danger and got lost in the forest; the other took the way of destruction, stumbled over a cliff and fell to his death.

Christian crawls up the hill.

I looked then at Christian as he went up the hill,
and noticed that he soon changed from running to
walking, and from walking to climbing on his hands
and knees, because of the steepness of the way.

Christian sleeps in the arbor.

About midway to the top of the hill was a pleasant arbor built by the Lord of the hill for the refreshment of weary travelers. Christian reached this place and sat down to rest. Taking the scroll from his bosom, he began to read, but being weary he soon fell into a deep sleep and the scroll fell out of his hand. As he was sleeping, one came and wakened him, saying, "Go to the ant, thou sluggard; consider her ways and be wise" (Prov. 6:6).

Timorous and Mistrust appear.

Christian suddenly started up and sped on his way till he came to the top of the hill. Here he was surprised to see two men coming toward him. The name of the one was Timorous, and the other, Mistrust. To them Christian said, "Sirs, what is the matter? You are going the wrong way."

They answered, "We saw lions in the way. The farther we go, the more danger we meet with, so we are going back."

Then said Christian, "You make me afraid. Which way shall I go to be safe? To go back to my own country is certain death. To go forward is fear of death, but there is everlasting life at the end of the road. I will go forward."

Christian misses the scroll.

So Mistrust and Timorous ran on down the hill, and Christian went on ahead. As he walked he thought he would read from the scroll for comfort. He felt in his bosom for it, but found it not. He was greatly perplexed until he remembered that he must have dropped it while he was sleeping in the arbor. Falling on his knees, he asked God's forgiveness, and then went back to look for the scroll.

Christian hastens after his scroll.

As he went back searching for his scroll, he sighed and wept with regret. "The Lord built that arbor only for the refreshment of pilgrims," he said. "How foolish and sinful I was to sleep in the midst of difficulty!"

He finds the scroll in the arbor.

When he reached the arbor, he sat down and wept
again. But at last, looking around sorrowfully, he
spied the scroll down under the bench. With trembling hand he snatched it and thrust it back into
his bosom. Who can describe the joy he now felt?
This scroll was his ticket to Heaven and his assur-
ance of eternal life!

Christian at Palace Beautiful.

How nimbly Christian now hastened up the rest of the hill! Yet before he reached the top, the sun had gone down. Again he bewailed the folly of his sleeping, for he remembered that Mistrust and Timorous had told of having been frightened by lions on the road ahead. He said to himself, "If these beasts come upon me in the dark, I shall be torn to pieces." But even as he repented of his mistake, he lifted up his eyes and saw before him a stately palace, the name of which was Beautiful.

Christian sees the lions.

So I saw in my dream that he hurried to the palace, hoping to get lodging there for the night. But before he had gone far, he entered a narrow passage and saw, a short distance ahead, two lions lying in front of the gate.

The gateman tells him the lions are chained.

"Now," he thought, "I see the dangers which
frightened Mistrust and Timorous." But the gateman, whose name was Watchful, seeing Christian halt
as if he would go back, cried out, "Why are you so
cowardly? Don't be afraid of the lions, for they are
chained and placed there to test your faith! Stay
in the middle of the path and no harm will come
to you."

Christian advances.

Then I saw Christian advance, trembling for fear of the lions. But he followed the gateman's directions, and though he heard the lions roar, they did him no harm. When he reached the gateman, he asked, "May I lodge here for the night?"

The gateman replied, "This house was built by the Lord of the Hill for the rest and safety of pilgrims. But where have you come from, and where are you going?"

"I came from the City of Destruction and I am going to the Celestial City. I pray that you give me a night's lodging."

"What is your name?"

"My name before was Graceless, but now it is Christian."

"Why do you come so late?"

The gateman inquired, "How do you happen to come so late? The sun is already set." Christian then told how he had fallen asleep in the arbor and how he had lost his scroll and had to return.

Watchful, the gateman, calls Discretion.

So Watchful, the gateman, rang a bell, at the sound of which a young woman named Discretion appeared and asked why she was called. Watchful introduced Christian, saying, "If it seems good to you, **may this man spend the night here?**"

Discretion questions Christian.

In answer to Discretion's questions, Christian told her how he had started on the journey and what experiences he had met with on the way. As Discretion listened, tears came to her eyes, and she said, "I will call other members of the family to meet you."

He meets the family.

So Discretion ran to the door and called for **Pru-**
dence, Piety and Charity. After they had talked with
Christian, they invited him to meet the rest of **the**
family. At the door, the whole family bowed and
welcomed him, saying, "Come in, thou blessed of
the Lord."

Prudence, Piety and Charity talk with Christian.
  He went with them into the house, and when he was seated they brought him something to drink. Prudence, Piety and Charity continued to talk with him until supper was ready. Far into the night they sat and talked about the Lord of the Hill. Then, after prayer, they separated and went to their rooms to rest.

The room called Peace.
They showed Pilgrim a large upper room called Peace, whose window opened toward the sunrise. Here Christian slept restfully until daybreak.

A library of rare and ancient books.

The next morning his friends told Christian he should not leave until they had shown him some records of greatest antiquity which gave the family history of the Lord of the Hill. These records proved He was the Son of God, without beginning and without end, that He had subdued kingdoms, and that He was ready to forgive those who had reviled Him. They also showed that He fulfilled all the prophecies concerning Him.

*Suits of armor for protection against
the wiles of the devil.*

The family next took him into the armory and
showed him all manner of armor, such as sword,
helmet, shield, breastplate, all-prayer, and shoes that
would not wear out (Eph. 6:11-18) . There were also
some engines of war, by means of which the warriors
of old had done brave deeds. Christian was delighted
with all these things.

They show him the Delectable Mountains.

When he would have continued his journey, they encouraged him to stay another day, saying, "If the day be clear, we will show you the Delectable Mountains." So he consented. The next morning, they took him to the housetop and bade him look south. There he saw, at a great distance, a most pleasant country beautified with mountains and woods. "That is Immanuel's Land," they said. "When you get there, some shepherds will point out to you the gates of the Celestial City."

They keep him no longer.

Now Christian desired to set out immediately, so they did not keep him any longer.

Christian puts on the armor.

"But first," they said, "let us go again into the armory where you can put on the whole armor of God, lest you meet with the assaults of the enemy on the way."

After he had put on his armor, he walked with his friends to the gate. There he asked Watchful if he had seen any pilgrims passing by.

"Yes," said the gateman, "a man named Faithful passed by. But by now he has already gone down the hill."

"Oh," replied Christian happily, "I know him. He is my townsman, my near neighbor. I must hurry and catch up with him."

Christian descends the Hill Difficulty.

As Christian started out, Discretion, Piety, **Chari**-
ty and Prudence insisted on accompanying him. So
they walked on together talking about the Saviour.
When they started down the hill, Christian said, "It
was difficult coming up, and so far as I can **see it**
is dangerous going down."

"Yes," said Prudence, "so it is. It is hard **for a**
man to go down into the Valley of Humiliation,
where you now are headed, and not have an **acci**-
dent on the way. That is why we are accompanying
you."

113

His friends give him gifts.

At the foot of the hill, his friends gave Christian in parting a bottle of wine, a loaf of bread and a cluster of raisins. He received these gifts thankfully and went on his way alone into the Valley of Humiliation.

Christian becomes aware of Apollyon.

In the Valley of Humiliation, poor Christian was hard put to it. He had gone but a little way when he saw a foul fiend whose name was Apollyon. Then Christian began to be afraid and to wonder whether he should go back or stand his ground. So he went on, and Apollyon met him.

115

The hideous monster, Apollyon.

The monster was hideous to behold. He was clothed with scales like a fish, had wings like a dragon, feet like a bear. Out of his mouth, which was as the mouth of a lion, he breathed fire and smoke. He was the king of the City of Destruction and he meant to kill Christian.

Apollyon claims Christian.

APOLLYON: You are one of my subjects, for I am the prince and god of the City of Destruction. Why have you run away from your king? If I did not hope that you would still serve me, I would strike you to the ground.

CHRISTIAN: I was indeed born in your kingdom, but your service was hard. A man cannot live on your wages, for "the wages of sin is death." I have now joined myself to the King of princes. I like His service, His wages, His servants, His country and company better than yours. Do not try to persuade me. I am His servant and will follow Him.

Apollyon is angered.

These resolute words angered Apollyon. In a rage
he threw a fiery dart at Christian's breast, but Christian's shield protected him. He quickly drew out the
Sword of the Spirit and attacked Apollyon.

They struggle for half a day.

The two opponents struggled back and forth for half a day without either gaining the advantage. Christian, whose head and feet were wounded, had lost much blood. Unable to resist any longer, he fell to the ground, and his sword flew out of his hand.

Christian gives Apollyon a deadly thrust.

But just as Apollyon was about to kill him, Christian nimbly reached out his hand and grasped his sword, saying, "Rejoice not against me, O mine enemy: when I fall, I shall arise" (Micah 7:8). With that, he gave Apollyon a deadly thrust that made him draw back. "Nay, in all these things we are more than conquerors through him that loved us," (Rom. 8:37) cried Christian and came at him again.

Apollyon flies away.
Defeated, Apollyon spread his dragon's wings and
flew away. For a season Christian saw him no more.

Christian gives thanks.

All during the struggle Christian had been grim and sober. Not till he had succeeded in wounding Apollyon with his two-edged sword did he smile and look upward. Then said Christian, "I will give thanks to Him who delivered me out of the mouth of the lion and helped me against Apollyon."

Christian's wounds are healed.

Then there came a hand to him with leaves from the tree of life. Christian took them and laid them on the wounds he had received in battle, and he was healed immediately.

Christian satisfies his hunger.

He sat down to eat the bread and drink the wine that had been given him. Then, being refreshed, he resumed his journey with his sword in his hand, for he said, "Some other enemy may be near." But he met with Apollyon no more in the Valley of Humiliation.

The Valley of the Shadow of Death.

I saw in my dream that Christian came to the edge
of another valley called the Valley of the Shadow of
Death. Here, two men who were hurrying back
gave him an evil report of the dangers ahead. "The
valley itself is dark as pitch," they said. "We also
saw horrible fiends there and dragons of the pit,
and we heard a continual howling and yelling as of
people in misery." But Christian replied, "In spite
of what you say, this must be the way to the desired
haven."

Christian enters the valley.

Then I saw that the pathway through the Valley of the Shadow of Death was bordered on the left by a very deep ditch and on the right by a miry slough. The path itself was very narrow. As Christian would try to shun the ditch on the one side, he would almost tip over into the mire on the other. About the middle of the valley he came to the mouth of Hell, belching fire and smoke and roaring with hideous noises of fiends.

A new weapon — All-prayer.

Here Christian had to sheath his sword and take up a new weapon called All-prayer (Eph. 6:18). So he prayed, "O Lord, I beseech thee, deliver my soul." But the unseen fiends seemed to come nearer and nearer. When they were almost upon him, he cried out with a loud voice, "I will walk in the strength of the Lord God!" So they turned and came no farther.

Christian reviews his journey.

When morning came, he looked back to see what hazards he had gone through in the dark. He saw clearly the deep ditch on the one hand and the miry bog on the other, and also how narrow was the path between. Afar off he saw the foul fiends and dragons, but after daybreak they dared not come near.

Christian sees Faithful.

Now Christian went on his way till he came to
a little hill in the valley from which he could view
all sides. Seeing Faithful ahead of him, he cried out,
"Wait for me!" But Faithful answered, "I dare not
stop because the avenger of blood is behind me."

Christian boasts of his speed.

Christian was annoyed to hear this and ran with all his might till he overtook Faithful. Smiling conceitedly and forgetting to watch his step, he stumbled and fell.

Faithful helps him.

Seeing him fall, Faithful ran up and helped him to his feet. Then they went on very lovingly, talking together about all that had happened to them on their pilgrimage.

Talking together, they walk the way to Zion.

CHRISTIAN: How long did you stay in the City of Destruction before you set out after me?

FAITHFUL: Till I could stay no longer. I had hoped to go along with you, but you got away ahead of me, so I had to go on alone.

CHRISTIAN: Did you hear any news of neighbor Pliable?

FAITHFUL: Since he went back many of the neighbors have made fun of him and despised him.

CHRISTIAN: Didn't you talk with him before you left?

FAITHFUL: I met him once in the street, but he sneaked off on the other side as though ashamed of what he had done.

Faithful tells about meeting Wanton.

FAITHFUL: I did not fall into the Slough of Despond as
you did, nor did I meet with danger on the way to the narrow gate, but on the road I met with one named Wanton.
With flattering lips she promised me all kinds of pleasures,
but I shut my eyes so I would not be bewitched by her.
She railed on me, but I went on my way.

Adam tempts Faithful.

CHRISTIAN: Did you meet with any other dangers?

FAITHFUL: When I came to the foot of the Hill Difficulty I met a very old man who said he was Adam from the town of Deceit. He asked me to live with him and promised to make me his heir.

Adam's three daughters serve dainties.

FAITHFUL: I asked him what kind of house he kept and what servants he had. He told me he served all kinds of dainties on his table and that his servants were his own three daughters: the Lust of the Flesh, the Lust of the Eyes, and the Pride of Life (I John 2:16). He said I could marry them all if I desired. At first I was inclined to go with him, but I changed my mind.

135

Adam curses Faithful.

FAITHFUL: In a flash I realized that if he got hold of me, he would sell me as a slave. So I bid him cease talking, for I would never go to his house. Then he cursed me and said he would send someone to trouble me. As I turned to leave him, he took hold of me and gave me such a wrench I thought he would tear me apart. This made me cry, "O wretched man that I am!" (Rom. 7:24). So I went on my way up the hill.

"A man overtook me."

FAITHFUL: When I was just about halfway to the top
of the Hill Difficulty, I looked around and saw a man
following me swift as the wind. He overtook me just as
I reached the arbor.

"He knocked me to the ground."

FAITHFUL: The man came up to me and with a lash of his whip knocked me to the ground where I lay as though I were dead. When I came to myself again, I asked him, "Why did you treat me so cruelly?" He replied, "Because of your secret liking for Adam." With that he struck me another blow on my breast and beat me down again. When I revived once more, I cried, "Have mercy and spare my life!" Doubtless he would have made an end of me except that one came by who bade him desist.

Faithful recognizes his benefactor.

CHRISTIAN: And who was he that bade him cease?

FAITHFUL: I did not know Him at first, but as He went by I saw the nail holes in His hands and knew He was our Lord.

CHRISTIAN: He that overtook you was Moses. He spares none and shows no mercy to those that transgress the law.

Discontent.

CHRISTIAN: Tell me, did you meet with anybody in the Valley of Humiliation?

FAITHFUL: Yes, I met Discontent who tried to persuade me to return with him. He said the Valley of Humiliation was entirely without honor. I answered him, "Before honor is humility, and a haughty spirit before a fall" (Prov. 15:33; 16:18). I would rather listen to the wise men of old and choose humility than seek what you call honor.

Shame accosts Faithful.

CHRISTIAN: Did you meet with anyone else in that valley?

FAITHFUL: Yes, I met Shame, a man with the boldest face I ever saw. He certainly was wrongly named. He said it was a low, sneaking business for a man to mind religion, and that pilgrims of the heavenly way are all lowly, inferior people. Among other things, he said it is a shame to ask forgiveness or to make restitution.

Faithful answers.

CHRISTIAN: What did you say to him?

FAITHFUL: At first I could not think what to say, but then I remembered that "that which is highly esteemed among men is abomination in the sight of God" (Luke 16:15). So I said, "Those who make themselves fools for the sake of the kingdom of heaven are the wisest after all. If I left my Lord and followed you, how could I dare look Him in the face at His coming?" So when I had shaken him off I went on my way singing.

Here comes Talkative.

Moreover, I saw in my dream as they went on, Faithful chanced to look to one side and saw a man named Talkative walking nearby. Faithful went over and spoke to him, "Friend, are you also going to the heavenly country?"

"Yes," Talkative answered, "I am going to the same place.'

"Let us go together," said Faithful, "and spend the time talking about profitable matters."

Christian advises Faithful.

After they had talked together for a while, Faithful went over to Christian and said softly, "What a brave companion we have."

But Christian answered, "Let me tell you about that fellow. I know him well, for he lives in our town. His name is Talkative, the son of Say-well, and he lives on Prating Row. He has a clever tongue and is full of fine words, but religion has no place in his heart."

FAITHFUL: Then I am greatly deceived in this man. How shall we get rid of him?

CHRISTIAN: Take my advice. Start a discussion on some serious subject, and then ask him plainly whether his faith is real or just a matter of talk. You will find him to be as sick of you as you are of him.

Faithful tests Talkative.

So Faithful stepped aside and said to Talkative, "How is it now?"

TALKATIVE: Thank you, well. I thought we should have had a long talk by this time.

FAITHFUL: If you wish, let us talk about this question. How does the saving grace of God show itself in the human heart?

They discuss sin and grace.

TALKATIVE: That is a good question. First, grace causes a great outcry against sin.

FAITHFUL: I think you should rather say it causes the soul to hate sin.

Talkative fails the test.

TALKATIVE: Why, what difference is there between crying out against sin and hating it?

FAITHFUL: A great deal. I have heard many cry out against sin in the pulpit who enjoy it in the heart and in the home. Is your religion only in word and speech or is it in deed and truth?

At that Talkative got red in the face and asked, "Why do you ask me such a question?"

Faithful and Talkative part company.

FAITHFUL: Because you are so ready to talk. But with you, drinking, covetousness, swearing, lying and religion all stand together.

TALKATIVE: Since you are so ready to judge me, I conclude that you are a peevish pessimist not fit to converse with. So I bid you good-by.

"From such withdraw thyself."

Then up came Christian and said to his brother, "I told you how it would be. Your words and his lusts could not agree. He would rather leave your company than reform his life. He has saved us the trouble of leaving him, for he would only have been a blot on our company. Besides, the apostle Paul says, 'From such withdraw thyself'" (I Tim. 6:5).

Christian commends Faithful.

FAITHFUL: I am glad we had this little talk with him. I have spoken plainly; if he refuses to repent, I am clear of his blood.

CHRISTIAN: You did well to talk so plainly. I wish that all men would speak in such a way. Then would men either learn to be sincere or they would be uncomfortable in the company of saints.

They walk and talk together.

Walking and talking together along the way, the two pilgrims found the long journey pleasant and profitable. Otherwise, it would have been tedious, for they were going through a wilderness

They meet Evangelist.

When they were almost out of the wilderness, they chanced to look back and saw a familiar figure. "It is my good friend Evangelist!" cried Christian.

EVANGELIST: Peace be with you, my friends. How have you fared since we last parted?

Christian and Faithful told him all things that had happened to them on the way.

EVANGELIST: How glad I am, not that you have met with trials, but that you have been victorious. An incorruptible crown is before you. So run that you may obtain it. Above all, look well to your own hearts and set your faces like flint. You have all power in heaven and earth on your side.

Evangelist warns of dangers ahead.

CHRISTIAN: Thank you, Evangelist, for your encouraging words. Since you are a prophet as well as an evangelist, tell us more about the road ahead and how we can resist and overcome the dangers.

EVANGELIST: My sons, you have heard that you must through much tribulation enter into the kingdom of God (Acts 14:22). As you see, you are almost out of the wilderness. You will soon come to a town where you will be attacked by enemies who will try to kill you, and one or both of you will seal your testimony with your blood. But be faithful unto death, and the King will give you a crown of life (Rev. 2:10).

The pilgrims approach Vanity Fair.

Then I saw in my dream that when they were out
of the wilderness they came to the town of Vanity.
In this town there is a fair held, called Vanity Fair.

Vanities are sold here.

Now Vanity Fair is no new business. Long ago, Beelzebub, Apollyon and Legion saw that pilgrims going to the Celestial City must pass through the town, so they contrived to set up a permanent fair in which would be sold vanities such as worldly honors and carnal delights.

A hubbub arises over the pilgrims.

As the two pilgrims approached the fair, all the
people were stirred, and a hubbub arose. Because
the pilgrims' clothing was not like that of the towns-
people, everyone stared at them, judging them to be
fools or madmen. Also, since they spoke the language
of Canaan, they seemed like barbarians to the men
of this world who kept the fair.

The pilgrims refuse the vanities of the fair.
They valued lightly the wares that were offered
for sale, and when the merchants called on them
to buy, they covered their ears and cried, "Turn
away mine eyes from beholding vanity."

A merchant mocks them.

One merchant, beholding the behavior of the strangers, mocked them, saying, "What will you buy?" But they looked gravely on him and answered, "We buy the truth." This caused him to despise the pilgrims more than ever.

The crowd abuses them.

Such an uproar was stirred up in the street that
all order was lost and the crowd began to abuse the
pilgrims. Some mocked, some taunted, and some
called on others to strike them. At last word was
brought to the head of the fair.

Taken into custody and questioned.

Christian and Faithful were taken into custody for questioning. In answer to the questions the two said, "We are pilgrims and strangers in the world and are on our way to our own country, the heavenly Jerusalem."

The examiners beat them.

But the examiners, believing them to be either mad or deliberately stirring up trouble, beat them and smeared them with mud.

They are put in a cage.

Then they put Christian and Faithful into an
iron cage as a public spectacle to everyone. The two
lay there, objects of jeering and spite, and there was
no one to defend them. The head of the fair laughed
loudly at all that befell them.

Their accusers fight among themselves.

But the pilgrims endured patiently, giving good for bad and kindness for injuries done. Some men in the fair, less prejudiced than the rest, began to rebuke the others for their abuses. But the latter turned on them in anger and both sides fell to fighting among themselves.

*Christian and Faithful are accused of
causing the disturbance.*

"Beat them with rods!"

They are also put in chains.

A trial is ordered.

But Christian and Faithful behaved themselves so wisely and bore their shame with such **meekness** that even more men were won over to their side. This so enraged the opposing party that they determined to have the pilgrims put to death. So a trial was ordered.

Faithful prepares to defend himself.

They were brought to trial before Judge Hate-good. The charge was as follows: "These men are enemies of trade and disturbers of the peace. They have made divisions in the town and have won over a party to their dangerous opinions, in contempt of the law of our prince."

But Faithful rose up and defended himself, saying, "I have only set myself against that which opposes the law of Him who is higher than the highest. The prince you speak of is Satan, the enemy of our Lord, and I defy him and all his devils."

The three witnesses.

Judge Hate-good announced that anyone having a complaint against the prisoners should appear and give evidence. So there came in three witnesses: Envy, Superstition and Famehungry.

Faithful again speaks boldly.

These three men accused Faithful of ruining their trade by saying that Christianity and the customs of Vanity Fair could not be reconciled and by talking against their prince, Satan, and his friends.

But Faithful again boldly defended himself, saying, "I have been falsely accused. I did say that whatever is against the Word of God is opposed to Christianity, and that divine faith is required in the worship of God. So far as the prince of this town and his rabble are concerned, they are more fit for hell than here. And so the Lord have mercy on me!"

The verdict — guilty.

Then the judge charged the jury to bring in a
verdict, whether to execute Faithful or to set him
free. The members of the jury were Mr. Blindman,
Mr. Reject-good, Mr. Love-lust, Mr. Live-loose, **Mr.
High-mind**, Mr. Hate-light, Mr. Liar, Mr. Enmity,
Mr. Headstrong, Mr. Cruelty, Mr. Hold-a-grudge and
Mr. Malice. They had already passed judgment
against him in their hearts, so they were not long in
bringing in the verdict of guilty.

He is sentenced to die.

Judge Hate-good ordered that Faithful be taken
to the execution ground to receive the most cruel
death their law could devise.

They strip Faithful.

173

They scourge him.

174

They buffet him.

They stone him, and slash him with knives.

They pierce him with swords.

They burn him at the stake.
Last of all they bound him to a stake and burned
him to ashes. Thus Faithful came to his end.

Faithful arrives at the Celestial City.
Then I saw in my dream that, though Faithful
had been cruelly burned at the stake, at the **moment
of death** he was carried aloft through the **clouds di-**
rectly to the Celestial City gate.

Christian escapes and is joined by Hopeful.

Christian was taken back to prison where he remained for a time. But God who overrules all, so wrought that Christian escaped and went on his way. He was not alone, for he was joined by a man named Hopeful who had been moved by the noble example of the pilgrims.

They journey together.

The two men entered into a brotherly covenant to walk the heavenly way together. Hopeful told Christian there were many other men of Vanity Fair who would some day follow them.

The pilgrims meet By-ends (*Love-gain*).

Shortly after they left the fair, the two pilgrims overtook a man on the road and asked him where he came from and how far he was going. "I come from the town of Fair-speech and am going to the Celestial City," he answered, but he told them not his name. However, he claimed that he was related to all the rich and noble families in Fair-speech. "We differ in religion from some in two small matters," he said. "We never strive against wind and tide, and we are most zealous when religion walks in silver slippers."

"Are you Mr. Love-gain?"

Guessing who the man was, Christian asked, "Are you not Mr. Love-gain?"

LOVE-GAIN: That is not my real name; it is a nickname given me by some who do not like me. If you take me along, you will find me a good companion.

CHRISTIAN: If you go with us you must go against wind and tide, and you must also own religion in rags as well as in silver slippers.

Mr. Love-gain is joined by three others.

But Love-gain refused to accept these terms and
the two pilgrims parted company with him. As they
left him they saw that he was joined by three others
— Mr. Hold-the-world, Mr. Money-love and Mr. Save-
all. They all bowed and greeted one another with
flattering words. The four had been fellow students
in the school of Mr. Gripe-man, who had taught
them to attain success by violence, by flattery, by
lying, or by putting on a guise of religion.

Love-gain and his companions discuss the pilgrims.

Love-gain talked to his companions about **Christian** and **Hopeful**, saying, "They don't understand how to profit by changing with the times. They don't wait for wind and tide, but rush on their journey in all kinds of weather. They hazard all for **God**. As for myself, I am for taking precautions to secure my life and property. I shall profess religion only as long as the times and my personal safety warrant it."

They question the pilgrims.

Catching up with the pilgrims, the men asked them the question: "Suppose a man should be offered a chance to get the blessings of this life, but in order to secure them he must appear to become very religious. May he not use this means to attain his end, and yet be an honest man?"

Christian answered, "Even a babe in religion could answer ten thousand such questions. If it is unlawful to follow Christ for loaves, how much more abominable it is to make religion a stalking-horse to gain and enjoy the world."

Christian and Hopeful go on ahead.

The four stood staring uncomfortably at each other. Being unable to reply to Christian, they fell behind and let the pilgrims go on ahead. Then said Christian to his fellow, "If these men cannot stand before the sentence of men, what will they do before the sentence of God?"

Demas and the Hill called Lucre.

Now Christian and Hopeful quickly outdistanced the four and came to a Hill called Lucre containing a silver mine. A little to the side of the road stood a man named Demas (II Tim. 4:10) who called to them, "Ho! turn aside and I will show you something."

188

Pilgrims refuse to turn aside.

The pilgrims would not be tempted to turn aside, and they went on their way. But Love-gain and his companions, at the first call, went over to **Demas** and were never seen again in the way.

The two pilgrims find an ancient monument.

I saw that the pilgrims came to a place where stood an old monument of strange form. It seemed to them like a pillar in the shape of a woman. On the pillar was an inscription in an ancient script which Christian was able to decipher. It read: "Remember Lot's wife." They both concluded that this was the pillar of salt into which Lot's wife was turned because she looked back with a covetous heart as she was fleeing from ancient Sodom.

The Pilgrims come to a pleasant river.

I saw that they went on their way to a pleasant river. As their road lay along the river bank, Christian and his companion walked with great delight. They drank of the sparkling water, sampled the many kinds of fruit and slept safely in a green meadow full of fragrant lilies.

They turn aside into By-path Meadow.

They were sorry when they had to leave the pleasant river and go back to the rough, stony highway. Their souls were discouraged because their feet were sore from the long journey. They longed for an easier way. A little before them, on the left hand, was a lush green meadow, called By-path Meadow. Seeing a grassy path running through the meadow parallel to the road, they could not resist the temptation to follow it.

Vain-confidence.

This path was easy to their feet, and they walked blissfully along till they met a man named Vain-confidence. He told them the path led to the Celestial City, so they followed him. But, alas, night came on and the sky grew dark. Vain-confidence, walking ahead, missed the path, fell into a deep pit and was dashed to pieces.

Lost in a storm.

The two pilgrims called to Vain-confidence, but groans were the only answer they heard. Then it began to rain and thunder; lightning flashed in a dreadful manner and the water rose fast. They searched but could not find their way back to the highway. They soon learned it was easier to go out of the way than it was to return.

They fall asleep.

At last they came to a little shelter where they sat
down till daybreak; being weary, they fell asleep.

Captured by Giant Despair.

Now not far from this place was Doubting Castle,
which was owned by the huge and dreadful Giant
Despair. Walking up and down in the fields the following morning, the giant caught sight of Christian
and Hopeful asleep on his grounds. In a grim and
surly voice he bade them awake.

The giant drives them into Doubting Castle.
When he demanded of them what they were doing on his grounds, they told him they were pilgrims
who had lost their way. Giant Despair then seized
them for trespassing and drove them before him into
Doubting Castle.

He locks them into a dungeon.

The giant locked them up in a dungeon where
they lay for three days and three nights, sleeping
on stones and breathing the foul air. They were left
without a bite to eat or a drop to drink. Seeing
no hope of release, they began to despair.

The giant seeks his wife's advice.

After Giant Despair had gone to bed, he told his wife Diffidence (No-faith) that he had taken a couple of prisoners and cast them into his dungeon for trespassing on his grounds. She advised him that **he** should beat them without mercy.

The pilgrims beaten unmercifully.

In the morning Giant Despair went down to the
dungeon and beat the pilgrims so unmercifully that
they could neither help themselves nor turn over
on the floor. But they endured the suffering without
a word.

No-faith says, "Bid them destroy themselves."

The next night, hearing that the prisoners were still alive, No-faith advised her husband to bid them destroy themselves. So again Giant Despair went to them. He told them in a surly voice that they would likely never get out alive and that they had better take their own lives.

Christian and Hopeful comfort each other.

But Christian and Hopeful tried to comfort each other, and so continued throughout another day in their pitiable condition.

No-faith next counseled her husband to take them to the castle yard and show them the bones and skulls of those who had already been killed for trespassing.

The pilgrims view the skulls.

Though they were terrified at the fearful sight, the two pilgrims still refused to kill themselves, so Giant Despair threw them back into the dungeon and again consulted his wife, "I fear," she said, "that they have picklocks by means of which they hope to escape.

"I will search them in the morning," said the giant.

The key called Promise.

In the dungeon again, Christian suddenly exclaimed, "I just remembered I have a key called Promise! I believe it will open any lock in Doubting Castle."

"Take it out and try," said Hopeful.

Christian uses his key.

When Christian tried his key in the dungeon door
it flew open with ease, and Hopeful and Christian
both stole out. Opening the big iron gate, however,
was desperately hard. When it finally did open it
made such a creaking noise that it woke Giant
Despair.

Giant cannot pursue — the pilgrims escape.

As the giant jumped up, his legs gave way and
he fell down in a fit, so that he could not go after
them. The two pilgrims escaped and came to the
King's highway where they were safe once more.

OVER THIS S
IS THE WAY
DOUBTING CA
WHICH IS KEPT
GIANT DESPAIR
WHO D
HIS KING

They erect a pillar.

When Christian and Hopeful had passed back
over the turnstile, they felt they should do something to prevent other pilgrims from falling into
the hands of Giant Despair. They decided to erect
a pillar on which they inscribed the warning: "Over
this stile is the way to Doubting Castle, which is
kept by Giant Despair, who despiseth the King of
the Celestial Country, and seeks to destroy His holy
pilgrims."

Fruit and flowers on the Delectable Mountains.
The two pilgrims continued their journey till
they reached the Delectable Mountains which belong
to the Lord of the Palace Beautiful. Here they
strolled along leisurely, admiring the beautiful gardens and tasting the delicious fruit.

They meet four shepherds.

On top of the mountains shepherds were feeding their flocks. They were Knowledge, Experience, Watchful and Sincere. The pilgrims asked the shepherds about the mountains and told of their experiences. Taking the pilgrims by the hands, the shepherds led them to their tents. There they urged them to eat the food that was prepared and to stay a while in the Delectable Mountains.

The pilgrims visit Mt. Error.

In the morning the four shepherds invited the pilgrims to walk with them on the mountains. After they had walked a while, enjoying the pleasant view, they came to the top of a hill called Error. Looking down, they saw the bones of men who had been dashed to pieces by falling over the cliff on the far side of the mountain.

"What does this mean?" asked Christian.

The shepherds answered, "They are the bones of those who turned from the truth and so fell over the cliff to their death."

View from Mt. Caution.

Next the shepherds took them to the top of Mt. Caution. From there they could see men in the distance wandering blindly among the tombs.

"What is the meaning of this?" asked Christian.

"A little below these mountains, did you not see a stile leading into an adjoining meadow? That stile leads to Doubting Castle. The men you see once started on a pilgrimage, but because the highway was rough they went into the meadow and were captured by Giant Despair. He blinded their eyes and led them among the tombs, where they still continue to wander.

Tears of remembrance.
Christian and Hopeful looked at each other with tears in their eyes, but said nothing.

A byway to Hell.

Then I saw that the shepherds led them to a door
at the bottom of a hill. Opening the door they bade
them look in. There the pilgrims saw a dark pit
from which rose swirling clouds of smoke and noise
of fire. They smelled the fumes of brimstone and
heard the cries of the tormented.

"What is this?" asked Christian.

"This is the hypocrites' door, the byway to Hell,"
the shepherds answered.

The pilgrims look through the telescope.

By this time the pilgrims wished to go on, so the shepherds walked with them as far as a high ridge called Clear. Here the Shepherds said, "Let us show them the gates of the Celestial City through our telescope. But when the pilgrims tried to look, their hands shook so they could not see clearly. However, they thought they saw the gates and also some of the glory of the place.

The shepherds' farewell counsel.

As they were leaving, one of the shepherds gave them a map of the way; one bade them beware of the Flatterer; another warned them not to sleep on the Enchanted Ground; the fourth wished them Godspeed.

Ignorance.

Then I saw the same two pilgrims going down
the mountainside. At the foot of the mountains, on
the left, lies the country of Conceit from which a
crooked lane comes in and joins the highway. Here
they met with Ignorance, a very lively lad who came
out of that country. He was truly ignorant of the
truth, but he was very conceited and certain that he
knew everything. Christian and Hopeful tried in
vain to persuade him. Nevertheless he continued to
follow them.

Mr. Turn-away.

After a while the two pilgrims entered into a very dark lane. Here they saw a man, whom seven devils had bound with seven strong cords, being carried back to the door that opened into the pit. He was Mr. Turn-away who dwelt in the town of Apostasy. Now good Christian and Hopeful began to tremble.

Little Faith attacked by three sturdy rogues.
Christian tells about Little Faith being attacked
by the three rogues, Mistrust, Faint-heart, and Guilt.
Great-grace from Good-confidence town frightened
the three thieves away.

The man in a white robe.

So they went on, followed by Ignorance, till they
came to a place where the road forked. The two
pilgrims were uncertain which road to take. As they
hesitated a man in a white robe came to them and
asked why they stood there.

"Follow me," said the man.
When they told him, he said, "Follow me. I too
am going to the Celestial City."

He leads them out of the way.

So they followed him. But the road he chose twisted
and turned so that before long their faces were turned
away from the Celestial City.

Entangled in a net.

Before they were aware of it, he led them into a
net in which they became so entangled they knew
not what to do. With that, his white robe fell off
and they realized they had been tricked. But they
could not get out of the net, so they lay there crying
for a long time.

Then said Christian, "Did not the shepherd bid
us beware of the Flatterer? We have proved the
words of the wise man true: 'A man that flattereth
his neighbor spreadeth a net for his feet'" (Prov.
29:5).

Shining One with a whip.

After a long time they saw a Shining One coming toward them with a whip of small cords in his hand. He rent the net and let them out. Then he said, "That man you followed was the Flatterer, a false apostle who has transformed himself into an angel of light" (II Cor. 11:13,14).

He whips them soundly.

Then the Shining One commanded them to lie
down and he whipped them soundly to teach them
not to go astray again. Then he said, "Follow me,
that I may set you on the right road once more."

Mr. Atheist.

After a while they saw afar off one coming along the highway to meet them. His name was Atheist, and he asked them where they were going. "We are going to Mt. Zion, said Christian.

He ridicules their faith.

Then Atheist laughed loudly, saying, "There is no such place in this world as you dream of!"

"But there is in the world to come," said Christian.

"I have sought for that place a long time, but have not found it," said Atheist. "I am now going back to the things I cast away in hope of that which I found not."

But knowing that he was blinded by the god of this age, Christian and Hopeful turned away from him and continued on their way.

Dull and drowsy — Enchanted Ground.

The next place they came to was the Enchanted Ground. Because the air was heavy, Hopeful began to be very dull and drowsy and suggested taking a nap. But Christian reminded him the shepherd had warned them not to sleep here, but to watch and be sober. So, to keep themselves awake they discussed God's dealings with them.

Ignorance follows them.

They talk with Ignorance.

CHRISTIAN: Come along, man. Why do you stay behind?

IGNORANCE: I take pleasure in walking alone.

CHRISTIAN: How stands it between God and your soul?

IGNORANCE: I have good thoughts, a good heart, and a good life according to God's commandment.

"The Word of God says . . ."

CHRISTIAN: The Word of God says, "There is none righteous, no, not one" (Rom. 3:10). Your name is Ignorance because you are ignorant of Christ's righteousness and the results of saving faith.

IGNORANCE: I will never believe that my heart is bad. Your faith is not mine, but mine is as good as yours.

"I cannot keep pace with you."

CHRISTIAN: No man can know Jesus Christ but by the revelation of God the Father. Be awakened, see your own wretchedness and fly to the Lord Jesus. By his righteousness you shall be delivered from condemnation.

IGNORANCE: You go too fast. I cannot keep pace with you. You go on; I must stay behind for a while.

The pilgrims enter Beulah Land.

By this time the pilgrims were out of the Enchanted Ground and had entered Beulah Land where the air was very sweet and pleasant. Here they heard continually the singing of birds and saw the flowers appear on the earth. Here too the sun shone night and day.

They are within the sight of the city.

They found they were now within sight of the
city, and they met many Shining Ones walking in the
garden. Here they wanted for nothing, for they found
an abundance of all they had sought for on their
pilgrimage.

A closer view of the city.

Drawing near the city, they saw that it was builded of pearls and precious stones and that the street was paved with gold. They heard voices from out of the city saying, "Behold thy salvation cometh; behold, his reward is with him."

"Whose gardens?"

As they came nearer, there were orchards, vine-yards and gardens. "Whose gardens are these?" asked the pilgrims of the gardener who stood in the way.

He answered, "They belong to the King and are planted here for His delight and for the comfort of the pilgrims."

The pilgrims sleep.

The gardener then gladly took them into the vine-
yards and bade them enjoy the fruits. He also showed
them the King's walks and the arbors where He delighted to be. Here they tarried and slept.

The glory of the city.

Then I saw that when they awoke they set out again on their journey. But the reflection of the sun upon the city of pure gold was so glorious that they could not behold it with open face.

Two men in shining raiment.

As they went on, two men met them. They were dressed in clothing that shone like gold, and their faces shone as the light. These men asked the pilgrims whence they came. When they answered, they said, "You have only two more difficulties to meet with, and then you will be in the city." The two men accompanied the pilgrims till they came in sight of the gate.

They go down into the water.

Between the pilgrims and the gate was a river. There was no bridge to go over, and the water was very deep. The pilgrims were stunned at the sight, but the men that went with them said, "You must go through the water or you cannot go in at the gate." In obedience to the words of the men, Christian and Hopeful went down into the water with fear and trembling.

Christian begins to sink.

As they felt the waters closing over them, Christian began to sink and cried out to his friend, "I sink in deep waters; the billows go over my head!"

Hopeful encourages Christian.

Then said Hopeful, "Be of good cheer, my brother. I feel the bottom; it is sound."

But Christian replied, "Oh, my friend, the sorrows of death have encompassed me. I shall not see the land that flows with milk and honey." Then a horror of great darkness fell upon him.

Christian faints for fear.

Christian's heart fainted for fear that he would drown in the river and never enter the Celestial City, and he could neither remember nor talk any more of grace and peace.

Safe on the other side.

For a while Hopeful had all he could do to keep his brother's head above the water. Christian would not be comforted until he heard Hopeful say, "Jesus Christ makes thee whole!" Then they both took courage until they were gone over and felt the ground firm under their feet. On the other side they saw the two Shining Ones waiting for them. They saluted the pilgrims and said, "We are ministering spirits sent by the Lord to help."

Celestial City ahead; armor left behind.

Now I saw in my dream that the Celestial City stood upon a hill. The pilgrims went up the hill with ease, for they had the two Shining Men to lead them.

The heavenly hosts meet them.

As they were drawing toward the gate, behold a company of the heavenly hosts came out to meet them. To this company the Shining Ones said, "These are the men who loved our Lord when they were in the world, and have left all for His holy name."

245

The King's trumpeters.

There came out also at this time to meet them
several of the King's trumpeters who made heaven
echo with the sound of their melodious music. These
trumpeters saluted Christian and his fellow with ten
thousand welcomes. Thus the pilgrims came to the
gate.

Enoch, Moses and Elijah.

Then I saw that the Shining Ones bade them call at the gate, and when they did, Enoch, Moses and Elijah looked over the walls. To them it was said, "These pilgrims have journeyed here for the love they bear the King."

They hand in their certificates.

The pilgrims handed in their certificates which they had received at the narrow gate. These were carried in unto the King. When He had read them, He said, "Where are the men?"

"They are standing outside the gate," He was told.

Then the King commanded to open the gates and bring them in.

They receive harps and crowns.

Now I saw in my dream that Christian and Hopeful went in through the gate. And lo, as they entered they were transfigured, and they had raiment put on them that shone like gold. They were also given harps and crowns. I heard all the bells in the city ring for joy, and it was said unto them, "Enter ye into the joy of your Lord." I also heard the men themselves sing with loud voices: "Blessing, and honor, and glory, and power, be unto him that sitteth upon the throne, and unto the Lamb for ever and ever" (Rev. 5:13).

Ignorance is rowed over the river.

I turned to look back and saw Ignorance come up to the river. He got over with little difficulty, for Vain-hope, a ferryman, rowed him over in his boat.

Ignorance climbs the hill.

Ignorance likewise climbed the hill and came up to the gate, only he came alone, neither did any man welcome him.

He has no certificate.

When Ignorance knocked on the gate, the men who looked over the wall asked, "Where did you come from? What do you want?"

He answered, "I have eaten and drunken in the presence of the King and he has taught in our streets." Then they asked for his certificate. He fumbled in his bosom for one, but he found none.

The Shining Ones speak to the King.

So the angels went in and told the King that Ignorance had arrived. But the King spoke, "Take him out, bind him hand and foot and take him away."

Ignorance bound and cast out.

Then they took him up and carried him through the air to the door that I saw in the side of the hill, and cast him inside. Then I saw that there was a way to Hell even from the gates of Heaven.

So I awoke, and behold it was a dream.